The Oregon Trail™

hmhco.com

The text was set in Garamond.
The display text was set in Pixel-Western, Press Start 2P, and Slim Thin Pixelettes.
Illustrations by June Brigman, Yancey Labat, Ron Wagner, Hi-Fi Color Design, and
Walden Font Co.

ISBN: 978-1-328-55000-2 paper over board
ISBN: 978-1-328-54996-9 paperback

Printed in the United States of America
DOC 10 9 8 7 6 5 4 3 2 1
4500718758

The Oregon Trail™

1

THE RACE TO CHIMNEY ROCK

by JESSE WILEY

Houghton Mifflin Harcourt
BOSTON   NEW YORK

1850

Oregon City

OREGON TERRITORY

Three Island Crossing

CALIFORNIA

UTAH TERRITORY

Legend

Oregon Trail ⬅ ▬ ▬ ▬

TERRITORIES ▬▬▬▬

State Lines ▬▬▬▬
(Modern Day)

NEW MEXICO TERRITORY

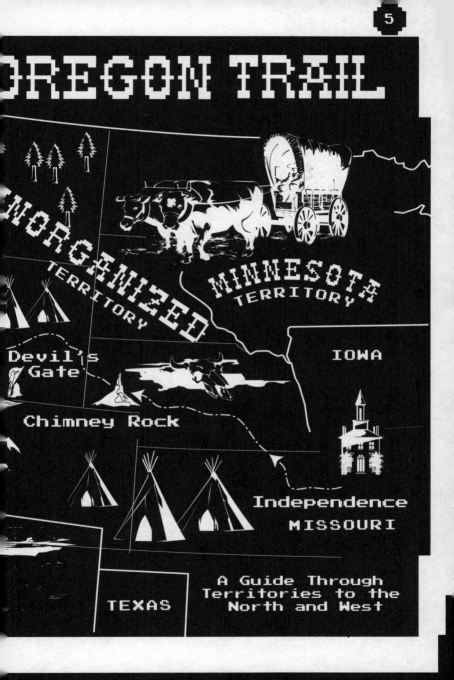

The Oregon Trail

GO WEST, Young Pioneer

You are loading up your covered wagon to head out to Oregon Territory, where a square mile of free farmland awaits your family. It's 1850 and there aren't any planes or trains yet, so you'll have to walk while your oxen pull your jam-packed wagon across North America's Great Plains, Rocky Mountains, and the lands of the many First Nations tribes, like the Otoe-Missouria, Osage, Cheyenne, Pawnee, Arapaho, and Shoshone.

For four to six months, you'll travel with a group of other families by wagon along a frontier path known as the Oregon Trail. Your first goal is to find your way to Chimney Rock on time. That's an important landmark, and if you can get to it in six weeks or less, you'll make it to the rugged mountains before the winter snows start to fall. But between you and Chimney Rock are wild animals, natural disasters, unpredictable weather, fast-flowing rivers, strangers, and sickness!

Only one path will get you safely across the prairie—and through this first book of four. There are twenty-two possible endings full of surprises, danger, and adventure.

You have to cross a wild river, how will you get across?

You're lost, what can you do?

You come face-to-face with a bear!

Your decisions along the way might send you somewhere unexpected, or put you at odds with other pioneers, or you might even end up a goner!

Before you start, be sure to read the *Guide to the Trail* on page 152. You'll make smarter decisions on your long journey if you know what to expect.

Sometimes, along the way, you'll get advice from guides, people from various Native American tribes like the Osage, Pawnee, and Otoe, or from Ma and Pa, but at other times, you'll have to trust only yourself to make the right decisions. Choose wrong and you'll never make it to Chimney Rock on time!

It's up to you!
What will you choose?

→ Ready? ←

LET'S BLAZE A TRAIL TO

CHIMNEY ROCK!

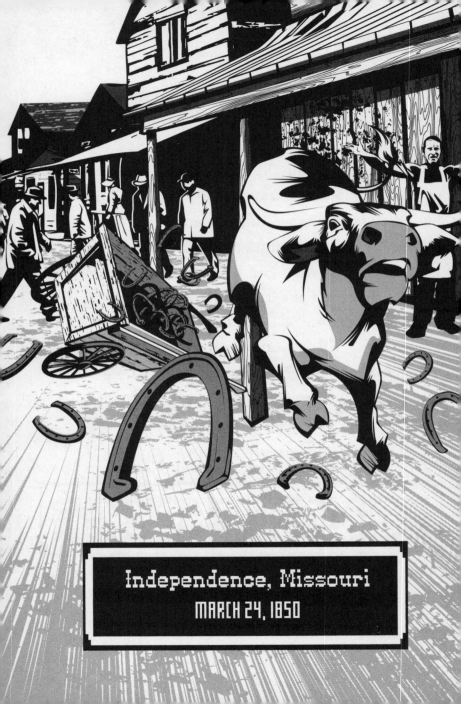

Independence, Missouri
MARCH 24, 1850

It's just after dawn, and you're asleep in the Frontier Inn in Independence, Missouri. You're dreaming when a noise jolts you awake.

SLAM! Clang! Clang!

You leap up and hurry to the window. What could be so loud this early in the morning?

You smile when you see that an ox has just knocked over a blacksmith's cart. Tools and horseshoes are spilled all over the dirt road. The blacksmith grumbles as he tosses horseshoes back into the cart.

Clang! Clang! Clang!

Now you're fully awake, so you stay by the window to watch the town come to life. You're amazed by all the activity you see. Carpenters are sawing wood. Shopkeepers are arranging barrels. And there as so many animals! Horses, cows, and huge oxen are all over.

You also see covered wagons, more than you've ever seen in your life. The wagons belong to the hundreds of families staying in town.

You're here with your family, your dog, your farm wagon, and your oxen. All of you, like the other families, are getting ready to start a five- to six-month journey to Oregon Territory. That's two thousand miles away on the other side of the continent! You'll have to walk alongside your wagon for nine hours a day, through prairies, deserts, and mountains. You gulp at the thought.

You turn and look back inside the room, at your family. Your brother and sister are still asleep, but Ma and Pa are already up and working. Ma is sewing a bonnet for your little sister Hannah, and Pa is making a slingshot for your younger brother, Samuel.

"Kentucky already feels very far away, doesn't it?" Ma says. You nod.

So far, the trip from your home in Kentucky has been pretty easy. You traveled from one town to the next, with comfortable breaks along the way. Soon, though, you'll be setting off on the Oregon Trail, where there won't be any big towns like Independence. You'll stay in tents instead of inns, and sometimes you'll sleep under the stars. It'll just be wide-open prairie for miles and miles, until you reach Chimney Rock. After that, you'll have to get over the mountains.

Pa comes to the window and puts his arm around you. His hands are rough from working as a carpenter.

"I've always wanted a farm of our own," he says. "Now is our chance."

"The land's free to families who head out West to claim it," Ma adds.

"Yes," Pa says, with a smile. "Just think of all the space we'll have."

You think of the cramped house you all shared in Kentucky. More space means plenty of room for all of you. And for your dog, Archie, to run around!

"Come here, boy," you call to Archie, then scratch him around the ears. He barks, waking up Samuel and Hannah.

Everyone washes up, and you head over to Jake's Tavern. The road is crowded with people and animals. Hannah holds on tight to your hand as you cross the street. You have to hop over oxen poop, and swerve to avoid a horse-drawn cart.

When you walk into the dining room at Jake's

Tavern, you're met by a strong scent of bacon, coffee, and fried eggs. The room is packed, and you squeeze around chairs to an empty wooden table in the back.

A group of men at the next table have a map spread out in front of them. They're pointing at landmarks with names like Devil's Gate and the Platte River.

You overhear stories about the terrible fates of unlucky pioneers that make you shiver. Luckily, Samuel and Hannah aren't listening. They're too busy slathering butter and syrup on their flapjacks.

Pa begins talking to the men with the map. They discuss whether to start down the Trail at the beginning of April next week, or to wait a little longer.

"If we leave now, we get a head start," one man says. "We'll get the best pick of land."

"But there isn't much grass for the oxen to graze on yet," another says. "We'd have to carry feed for them. It's better to wait a month."

"Waiting means more crowds on the Trail," the first man argues. "And if we're delayed, we might hit snow at the mountains after Chimney Rock."

Pa leans over and says to you, "There's a lot to consider. What do *you* think we should do?"

Your heart starts racing. This is a big decision, and you don't want to say the wrong thing.

"Go on," Pa says. "You're getting older now. Your opinion counts."

Pa really cares what you think. You feel honored.

You carefully consider the reasons for leaving next week or for waiting another month.

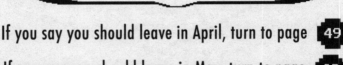

If you say you should leave in April, turn to page **49**

If you say you should leave in May, turn to page **62**

et's climb just a little higher," you agree. You pull
yourself onto the next ledge and see that your friend
Joseph was right. The view from Courthouse Rock is
truly spectacular.

You take a moment to look around, then you pull
out the pocketknife and carve your name into the
rock. It takes longer than you imagined, because you
have to be careful or you might cut yourself. You skip

adding the rest of your family's names because it's getting too dark out.

You start to make your way down the rock, as Joseph and Eliza scamper along below you. They both turn out to be pretty good climbers.

"Wait for me," you call out, as you hurry after them. But as you're speaking, you slip on a loose stone. You grab on to the rock and try to hold on. But you lose your grip and fall!

When you hit the ground, you hear a disturbing crunch. You can't feel your legs or move them at all.

Later, you learn that you've broken your back. You are lucky you didn't die. But your family's dreams have been crushed along with your bones. You will be carried to the next trading post in a sling hung between two oxen. But you won't go any farther on the Oregon Trail.

☞ THE END

You decide to get more food with your family's extra money. You, Samuel, and Ma head back to Wyatt's General Store.

"I'll take a fifty-pound bag of cornmeal," Ma says. "And some molasses."

"How about a few pounds of compressed vegetables?" the shopkeeper asks.

"Right," Ma says. "Add that, too."

Samuel looks at you and makes a face. You can't help but agree with him. The dried brown cake looks like something you might feed a horse.

With the extra food loaded onto the wagon, you're ready to head out early the next morning. Your wagon train includes ten other families and a captain named Caleb. Everyone is both nervous and excited.

Caleb gives the signal. "Westward ho!" he yells.

Pa touches the oxen lightly with his whip. The wagon starts to roll and you all cheer. You walk alongside the wagon, which is too full to ride in. Caleb keeps everyone moving at a steady pace, not too fast. But by midday, your legs are already tired, and you're ready for a break. You rest for an hour, which Caleb calls "nooning," but then it's time to move again.

At sundown, you finally stop after walking what must have been fifteen miles. Everyone is ready to make camp. You pitch the tent and Pa starts a fire. Ma mixes up some cornbread, and Hannah slices thick pieces of bacon. As you listen to it sizzle in the pan, your mouth starts to water. Even though everyone says you'll be sick of bacon soon, it tastes great tonight. Ma makes molasses pudding for dessert. You feel satisfied as you scrape the bottom of your tin plate.

The next morning, it's hard to get up at sunrise. You're drowsy when you sit down for breakfast, and you're still full from supper.

"You need to eat," Pa says. "You won't get another chance for hours."

So you force yourself to have some johnnycakes. You're glad Ma bought maple syrup.

You begin the day's hike, but your legs ache. It's going to take a while to get used to so much walking. You're relieved when the wagons arrive at the first trading post.

A Native man of the Osage tribe approaches and offers to be your guide from here to Fort Kearny, in exchange for some of your goods. He points at the molasses and syrup. Pa says the guide can help you ford rivers and hunt.

Then a merchant comes to talk to you. He says you can trade him things you don't really need for more important ones.

"You always need buckskins to repair shoes," he says. "And citric acid, which helps prevent sickness on the Trail." Then he adds, "I can take that molasses and syrup off your hands, too."

Both offers sound good. You'll be sad to see the molasses and syrup go, but a guide would be helpful. And so would the things the merchant is offering.

But you don't have enough to trade for both.

What does your family choose?

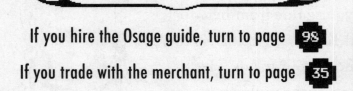

If you hire the Osage guide, turn to page **98**

If you trade with the merchant, turn to page **35**

You don't want Joseph's help, and you don't ask for it. You look over in his direction, and he smiles at you. But it doesn't seem like a friendly or sincere smile. It feels like he is waiting for you to mess up. You grab your little brother's slingshot and hop onto the wagon, climbing up to a flat spot above the sacks of flour. Bending your knees slightly, you shuffle a little and find your balance as the wagon rolls along.

A rabbit runs past, but it surprises you, and you aren't ready for it. So you draw your slingshot back with a rock in it, and wait for another. *There!* You see another rabbit sitting still, next to a small bush.

You take aim and then . . .

BUMP! Your wagon starts to move and hits a dip in the Trail. *Whoa!* You lose your footing, and then you tumble headfirst off the wagon. The oxen keep moving and don't slow down.

CRUNCH! One of the back wagon wheels rolls right over your leg. You cry out in intense pain, and pass out.

Your family has to travel back to Independence, Missouri, where a doctor sets your leg in a huge cast made of plaster of paris.

You won't be walking fifteen miles a day again for a very long time. If you're lucky, maybe your family can try the Oregon Trail again next year.

☞ **THE END**

You decide it's best to ford the Kansas River by heading straight through it rather than crossing diagonally. Stepping into the rushing current is a little frightening. *Brrrr!* The water comes up to your waist and it's freezing!

Pa needs you to help him steer the oxen. You're a stronger swimmer than Ma, so she sits in the wagon with Samuel and Hannah, who are too small to be in the water.

"Look at Archie go!" Pa laughs. Archie is the best swimmer in the whole wagon train. He paddles across the river like a champ, and seems to enjoy the swim.

Things start off well, but as you walk, the current grows stronger and stronger. It gets harder to fight it and still walk in a straight line. You wonder if this was the right choice, but now there's no way to change the plan. No one else can hear you over the rush of the river, and you don't want to get separated from the group.

You hit a rock and trip. *SPLASH!* You remember you were supposed to walk slowly, but it's hard to control your pace at all. You fall to your knees, then quickly try to stand back up, but you can't. You get pulled underwater by the current, and your shoulder hits the bottom of the river. When you try to stand up, the current pulls you back down. Water rushes down your throat, and you start to gag. No one hears your struggle over the sound of the rushing river.

By the time Pa turns around, and realizes you have vanished, it's too late. You drown.

☞ **THE END**

Your family decides to stay with the wagon train. Four other families leave with the soldier. With only six wagons in your train now, you move a little faster. But soon it starts to rain, and you slow down.

The rain pours down nonstop for the next two days. The oxen team is plodding through the mud, and you're squeezed inside the wagon with Samuel and Hannah. Even though Pa has rubbed extra linseed oil on the wagon's cover to seal it, water drips in through a few leaks. You feel damp and chilled.

Then the wagon comes to a halt. The oxen are still straining to pull it, but you're not moving.

"What's happening?" Hannah asks with wide eyes.

You stick your head out of the wagon and squint into the rain, looking for Pa. He's at the back of the wagon, shaking his head.

Ma walks up, rain dripping off her bonnet.

"We're stuck in the mud," she says. "We were slow already, but the wheels just sank in deeper."

The wagon ahead of you has the same problem. The oxen are pulling with all their might, but the wheels won't budge. Caleb walks over, his hair flattened with water.

"Half the wagons are stuck," he says. "We should have stopped before the path got so muddy."

"What now?" Ma asks.

"Well, we can wait out the rain," he says. "The oxen are getting exhausted. And if we keep trying to move, we might end up hurting them and damaging the wagons, too."

You look at the dark sky, covered with clouds. It doesn't look like the rain will ever stop.

"I can plug up the leaks on the wagons while we wait," Pa offers. "And we can try to find a drier spot."

Caleb nods, looking grateful.

"I saw a Pawnee settlement a ways back," Ma says. "Maybe they can help dig us out."

"We'd have to offer to pay them for their help," Caleb says. "Do you have extra food or money?"

Everyone starts talking about what to do. Some think it's better to wait out the rain. They are unsure about asking for help, and what it might cost. Others are eager to get moving toward Chimney Rock again, and are willing to pay for help.

What does your family decide to do?

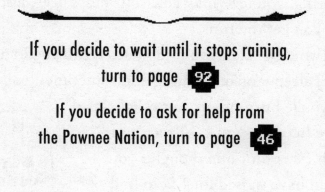

If you decide to wait until it stops raining, turn to page 92

If you decide to ask for help from the Pawnee Nation, turn to page 46

I'll just take a little drink of water while Ma boils the rest, you decide. You fill your tin cup halfway, and sip the water slowly. It feels good going down your throat, and you feel refreshed.

The next day, you feel a gurgling in your tummy as you're walking along, following your wagon tracks back toward the Trail. Then your stomach starts to ache a little. You can handle it at first, and you keep walking. But soon you start to get serious cramps. Sweating, you feel dizzy and your heart beats fast, and then you get the runs.

Two days later, you find yourself drifting in and out of sleep. You're sweating and sometimes, you feel like you're burning up, but other times you're freezing. You can't focus on much except for one thought: you should have waited for Ma to boil the water.

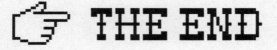

You die of dysentery.

 THE END

You decide people are more reliable than ropes. First, you help pull a trunk and some barrels out of the wagon to lighten the load. Then Pa and two others slowly back down the hill, bracing the wagon with their arms. The wheels are locked in place, so the wagon slides instead of rolling fast.

"Heave! Ho!" The men's muscles strain with the effort. But it works! They stop the wagon from sliding too quickly, and it descends safely down the steep slope. You help Ma lead the oxen down the hill over deep tracks made by other wagons.

"It's gorgeous here," Ma says. Ash Hollow is shady and filled with trees, grapevines, currant bushes, and flower blossoms. You think it's even nicer than Alcove Spring and the prettiest place you've seen since leaving Missouri over a month ago.

You gulp down refreshing spring water, while Samuel picks currants. They're sour, but Ma can cook with them.

You camp for two nights and get a good rest. The oxen rest, too, grazing on the plentiful grass. On the second night, Pa tells the family you will head out in the morning.

"I know it's hard to leave," he says. "But there's another surprise coming up soon."

"What is it?" Samuel asks, excited.

"I can't tell you," Pa says with a mysterious smile.

Soon you're back on the Trail, hiking again. But you recognize the surprise when you see it.

"Is that a . . . castle and a tower?" Hannah gasps, pointing to two huge rocks looming in the distance. They are bigger than any building you've ever seen. And they *do* look like a castle and a tower!

"No, those are Courthouse Rock and Jail Rock." Pa laughs. "No one knows how they formed, but they're important landmarks, and they are how we know we're going the right way."

"Can we get closer?" you ask, excited.

Getting closer means hiking an extra three miles, but everyone wants to do it.

As you near Courthouse Rock, you see it isn't smooth. The edges are jagged and rough. You crane your neck, but you can't even see the top.

"Look!" Joseph points. "People here before us carved their names into the rocks."

"Let's do it, too!" you say. "Can we?"

"Sure," Pa says. "It's tradition. Just be careful and be home for dinner."

You grab a pocketknife and head for the rocks, along with Joseph and Eliza. The sun is getting lower in the sky, which makes the rocks glow orange.

"Let's climb up a bit," Eliza says. "Lots of people's names are at the bottom. I want to carve mine closer to the top." You agree.

You start to scramble up the rock. You're having so much fun, you don't notice the sun starting to set at first.

"Maybe we should go back down," you say.

"Let's climb for a few minutes more," Joseph

protests. "I see a flat spot just a little higher. I bet it's got a great view. Let's carve our names there so no one else will carve over them."

You pause. You've come this far already, so surely a few more minutes won't hurt. You glance at the sky. Suppertime is approaching, and you want to be back before it gets dark. What do you decide to do?

If you agree to climb a little farther, turn to page **17**

If you insist on stopping where you are, turn to page **115**

You decide to trade your sweet goods for more important items.

"If you mix the citric acid with a little lemon and water, it tastes like lemonade," the merchant tells Ma.

"Won't fresh lemons be hard to find?" Ma asks.

"Well, you can use vinegar instead of lemons," he says. *Yuck!* You hope no one makes you drink that.

You look at the piles of supplies the merchant has. There is food of all sorts. You see every kind of tool and dish, from frying pans to knives. He even has a carved wooden chest of drawers.

"Where did all this stuff come from?" you ask.

"I traded for some of it," the merchant says proudly. "And I collect items people throw off their wagons. You'd be amazed by some of the crazy things people pack."

"Like what?" you ask.

"One family from New York brought along jars of fancy olives, and even some nice furniture. Once they hit the Trail, they realized they were overloaded. Then, they threw it off."

"And you just take it?"

"It's better than leaving it outside to rot," the merchant says. "In fact, I'll make you a deal. If you find me any good things, I'll buy them from you."

I can get back the molasses that way, you think.

You end up getting back your molasses and more. It turns out you're good at finding things people want. And you make really good deals, too!

Pretty soon you start selling to other people besides the merchant. Ma and Pa decide to set up a shop, and you trade things with pioneers passing through. With the endless stream of goods thrown away along the Oregon Trail, you earn lots of money.

There's no need to go any farther. You can make a fortune and buy land right here on the prairie. Maybe when you're older, there will be an easier way to get out West. Who knows, someone might even build a railroad one day.

☞ **THE END**

You wait for Ma to boil the water before you drink it, because she thinks the rotting branches and leaves that were in the water might make you sick. You're so thirsty, you gulp the water down while it's still warm. It doesn't taste great, and it still smells a little funny, but it quenches your thirst.

After eating and drinking, everyone is ready to get moving again. But now that your guide is gone, which way is the Oregon Trail?

Luckily, your wagon wheels have left deep ruts in the dirt. This is the first time you've been glad your wagon is so heavy!

You follow the wagon-wheel ruts back the way you came. After three long days, you find your way back to the Trail. A large wagon train is passing through. Pa speaks to the wagon captain, who agrees to let you join them.

Most of the people in your new wagon train seem really nice. But one man seems a bit aloof. You see him poking around your wagon during campfire.

"There's something strange about that man," you tell Ma. "He was near our wagon last night."

"Let's keep an eye on him, then," she says.

After what happened with Will, your whole family is a little less trusting of strangers. You decide to keep watching him.

That night, you see the man snooping around another wagon.

You wonder if you should say something to the wagon captain. What if you're wrong? You don't want to accuse an innocent person. But what if the man is taking things that aren't his?

If you tell the wagon captain what you saw, turn to page **66**

If you decide to wait until you know for sure, turn to page **100**

Fording the river seems like the best option. You'll save both money and time. First, Caleb sends in good swimmers with long sticks to scout ahead. They check to make sure the river doesn't suddenly get too deep.

"It's no more than two- or two-and-a-half feet deep all the way across," one swimmer says.

"But the current is strong," another warns. "We need to be careful and take small, slow steps to feel for the bottom without slipping."

Someone suggests you cross the river diagonally, heading downstream. That way you'll travel with the current, and the trip will be easier because you won't have to push back against the river. But you'll have to spend more time in the cold water, and you'll end up farther down the river than if you go straight.

Going straight across the river will be a shorter distance to cross. It'll save you time, but you'll have to work harder.

Everyone talks about which way is the best way to cross: straight ahead or on the longer, colder diagonal. What do you all decide?

If you go diagonally across the river, turn to page **127**

If you go straight across the river, turn to page **25**

Can't we just stay here, Pa?" you ask. "It'll sure be nice to take a break from the Trail."

"Yes," Ma chimes in. "It's so beautiful here. We couldn't ask for a nicer place to camp."

Pa shakes his head sadly. "But what about the dream?" he asks.

"We have plenty of time for our dream," you say. "But we're all so tired, and this is the perfect place to rest." As you speak, Hannah plucks yellow wildflowers from a plant and hands them to Pa. Samuel pulls berries off a bush and pops some in his mouth. He makes a face when they're tart.

Pa looks at all of you, and then he stares at the wagon. Finally, he laughs at Samuel's expression.

"I guess we can camp here for a while, while I rebuild the wagon," he says. "A lot of wagon trains pass through here. We can join another one in a few weeks or so."

You all help Pa clean up the mess of the wagon, and set up camp near the spring. The water is crisp and cool. It's the best you've ever tasted. Everyone feels a little better after washing up.

The next day, Pa cuts down a few of Ash Hollow's cedar trees. He makes planks to repair the wagon. It's nice to see him working as a carpenter again. He whistles as he hammers boards together. The extra wood comes in handy for firewood.

But after a while, you notice that the pile of wood is growing bigger and bigger, and the days are turning into weeks. Caleb and the rest of the wagon train are long gone.

"What's all that wood for?" you ask Pa.

"I'm making a log cabin," he says. "We can live in it as long as we want, and if we decide to leave, other pioneers can use it for shelter."

You look at Ma, and she smiles.

"Yes," she says. "Pa and I agree we don't need to go farther. We'll live here for as long as it makes us happy."

You see wagon trains come through, filled with dusty and exhausted travelers. Some of them need their wagons repaired. Pa does this in exchange for supplies. Ma sells some of her fruit pies, which soon become famous. And you are very happy in Ash Hollow. Sometimes dreams change. You wonder if you'll ever take on the Trail again.

☞ **THE END**

With the help of five strong Pawnee young men, your wagon is freed from the mud. Afteward, Pa and the oldest Pawnee man in the group smile and shake hands. Everyone offers the young men gifts, but they only accept a little food. One of them gives Hannah a small doll carved out of wood, which she clutches happily in her hands.

When Pa checks out your wagon, he notices the rear axle of the wagon is bent. It must have gotten damaged when the wheels were stuck.

"Thank goodness we brought those extra wagon parts," he says, getting to work to replace the axle. A few hours later, the rain finally stops and the sun comes out.

"The sunshine feels so good," Ma says, looking happier than she has in days. The group makes camp, and Ma starts a fire using lumps of dried buffalo poop called "buffalo chips." The hot meal is nice after days of cold biscuits and tough buffalo jerky. Your jaw still hurts from gnawing on that chewy dried meat.

The next morning you have to cross the Platte River. There's no ferry, but this river is tame and only a couple of feet deep.

"We can ford this pretty easily," Caleb tells everyone. He leads the horses and cows into the water first. Pa drives your team of oxen along. He walks through the water, but you ride in the wagon with Ma, Hannah, and Samuel. Pa did a good job plugging up the wagon leaks with candle wax and tar. Nothing gets wet, including you.

After you cross the river, Caleb says you're near a famous spot called Ash Hollow. It's known for its fresh water, berries, and trees. You haven't seen any of those for a week.

"I want berries!" Samuel says, and everyone agrees. You remember how nice the fresh water at Alcove Spring was, three weeks ago.

But getting to Ash Hollow will be a challenge. You have to make it down a steep hill without crashing your wagons. You talk about the best way to get the wagon train down safely, and you hear several different ideas.

"Maybe we can lower the wagons with rope," someone suggests.

"Or we can walk in front of them and brace them. We'd use our own strength to stop the wagons from sliding downhill," Pa says.

Both ideas might work. What does the group decide to do?

If you use ropes, turn to page **75**

If you use your own strength, turn to page **31**

I think we should head out next week," you say. "We can beat the crowds on the Trail and get to Oregon first. That way we can get the best land."

"I think you're right," Ma says.

Pa nods in agreement. "But we'll have to get a lot done quickly before then!" he says.

For the next week, everyone scrambles to get ready for the trip. You load up the rest of the wagon with food, clothes, camping gear, and tools.

Soon the wagon is overflowing with supplies for the long journey. On top of all that, Pa packs huge sacks of grain to feed the oxen. You need to carry it because the grass won't be long enough for them to eat for a few more weeks.

You've joined a wagon train with other families, and together you've all picked a captain named Caleb. He comes over and frowns at your wagon.

"That seems a bit overloaded," he says, looking worried. "Do you think your oxen team can pull it?"

"These oxen are young and strong," Pa says. "I've tested them out, and I think they can do it."

"All right," Caleb says. "We push out tomorrow!"

⭐ ⭐ ⭐

You've been on the Trail for two weeks now. At first, everything went well. Your wagon train moved at a good pace. The oxen had a lot of energy, covering about fifteen miles a day, and you managed to keep up with them.

But now, things are different. Everything hurts. Your legs, feet, and lower back are sore from walking. And you have blisters on your feet. Every time you take a step, you wince. You look at Hannah and Samuel trudging alongside you. They look just as miserable as you.

You really want to rest on the wagon, but Pa says every extra pound makes it harder on the oxen. And besides, there's little room left in the wagon with all the supplies.

"I want to ride on the wagon," Samuel whines.

"I can't walk anymore," Hannah declares. "My feet don't want to move another step."

Ma looks worried. "Maybe we should unload some of the things we don't need right now," she says. "I've seen flour sacks, bacon, and even an iron stove on the side of the Trail. People must have thrown them off their wagons."

"But we paid for all of these things," Pa protests. "If we push on to the next trading post, we can swap them for something else."

"The kids are so tired of walking. And the load is too heavy for the oxen," Ma says.

"What do you say, kids?" Pa asks. "It's not much farther. Can you make it to the trading post?"

He asks the three of you. But since you're the eldest, Hannah and Samuel will follow your lead. What do you say?

If you say you want to unload some extra supplies now, turn to page 83

If you say you can keep walking to the trading post, turn to page 112

Caleb, can I show you something?" you say.

"What is it?" Caleb sounds a little annoyed now.

"See that tree with the fallen branch and moss on one side?" You point. "We passed it yesterday."

"I don't think so," Caleb says.

A man from another wagon hears you and comes closer. "I noticed that, too," he says. "But I thought my mind was playing tricks on me."

Caleb gets upset, and he and the man argue. You watch Caleb sweat and turn red in the face. Finally, he throws up his hands, and furiously turns to you.

"If you think you know better, then you figure it out. Find yourselves another wagon captain!"

You are stunned. Caleb has been a great wagon captain so far, but now you have pushed him away. He wants to disband the wagon train and leave. Some families agree with him, while others agree with you.

Everyone pleads for him to reconsider, but Caleb's mind is made up. You look at Joseph and Eliza, who just shake their heads sadly at his stubbornness.

Half the group follows Caleb. The other half has heard gold is up for grabs in California. They'll make their own train, and follow the California Trail.

Your family doesn't really have a choice, since Caleb doesn't want you around. It looks like you'll be panning for gold soon . . . that is *if* you manage to make it out to California.

 **THE END**

He'll wait for the ferry," Ma says firmly.

Caleb nods his head in agreement. "It's decided," he says. "We'll camp here for the next few days. And in the meantime, we can hunt and fish to stock up on extra food."

Samuel claps his hands. He'd been the pickiest eater out of all of you.

You help Pa set up the tent, and then you roll out your mat and blanket. The wagons are all lined up in a semi-circle along the riverbank, which Caleb refers to as a "corral."

"This way the animals are protected from bandits," Pa had explained to you earlier. "And the corral stops them from straying off. See how the wagons form a fence?"

The next day, Pa and some other men hunt for buffalo. You and the other kids head out to search for fruit near camp.

"Look at these!" Hannah cries out. She points to a bush full of big, juicy blackberries. You're surprised, because Caleb had said berries wouldn't be ripe yet, but these are tender and juicy. You fill your tin cup until it's overflowing. And after Ma says the berries are safe to eat, you fill your mouths, too. Everyone's lips turn purple from the sweet juice. A few hours later, Pa and the hunters return with a bigger prize. Three buffalo!

That night, thick buffalo steaks sizzle on the cast-iron pan over the campfire. You feel lucky as you sink your teeth into the juicy meat. Dessert is even more delicious. Ma has used the sweet-and-tangy blackberries to whip up a warm cobbler with a crumbly bread topping. You look around, and everyone seems just as satisfied as you. You're pretty sure they are all glad to have waited for the ferry.

After dinner, you help Ma round up the oxen that have been grazing nearby, outside the corral. You count five, but your family owns six. *Where did the last ox go?*

"Is that a bell?" Ma asks. You strain your ears, and hear the faint tinkling of a distant cowbell. It must be the missing ox.

"Yes," you say. "He must have wandered away. I'll go fetch him while you take the rest of the team back to camp."

You walk in the direction of the sound, and stop to listen again. The cowbell is quiet now, but you do hear rustling. You head farther into the woods. Suddenly you see the shape of the missing animal. *Phew!* But wait . . . it has a leather rope around its neck. And it's being led away by a Native American boy not much older than you!

Your heart starts to pound wildly. Is this boy stealing your ox?

For a moment you freeze, uncertain of what to

do. Should you run back to camp and tell your family that your ox is being stolen? Or should you try being friendly by calling out to the boy? Maybe he'll just give the ox back.

What do you do?

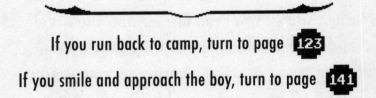

If you run back to camp, turn to page **123**

If you smile and approach the boy, turn to page **141**

Pa, look at those wagon ruts," you say to your
father. "See? They're going the other way."

"Are you sure?" Pa asks with a surprised look.

"Caleb led us in a circle," you continue. "We
should be going in the direction of those tracks."

Pa stops to inspect the wagon ruts.

Another man nods his head. "I think you're right.
I was wondering the same thing myself. Maybe Caleb
is confused or maybe his compass is broken."

"I already tried to tell him I thought so," you say.

"Well, we'll all have to talk to him again," the
man says firmly. "We need to stay on the Trail."

That night, when you camp, the man takes Caleb
aside. You see Caleb get upset, but then he calms
down and agrees to let you lead the way.

The next morning, you follow the wagon ruts.
You hike until late afternoon and come across a
trading post set back in a small canyon. Perfect! But
as you get closer, you realize it is abandoned. The
wind is howling and it gives you a spooky feeling.

And, mysteriously, the wagon ruts just stop. It's as if the pioneers who went down this path just vanished!

"Now what would you like us to do?" Caleb asks you, clearly annoyed by your interference.

You look at Pa and the other man. No one knows what to say.

Finally, Pa speaks.

"It's getting late, so I guess we'll make camp," he says. "Tomorrow, we'll head back the way we came and try to find the Trail."

No one uses the word "lost," but you know you are, even worse than before. You try not to think about it as you fall asleep to the howling wind, but fear grips your heart.

WHOOSH! You feel a flash of heat and wake to roaring flames. The campsite is burning! The animals start to panic, and everyone is screaming and scrambling to put out the fire. Ma and Pa throw pails of water, while others try to smother it with blankets.

By the time the fire is out, half the camp is destroyed. Three wagons are burnt down to the wheels. Your faces are covered with soot, and you

can't stop coughing from the smoke. But luckily, everyone is alive.

No one can figure out how the fire started. But the bigger problem is how you're going to get anywhere now.

☞ **THE END**

I think we should wait till May," you say. "We'll move faster if the oxen don't have to carry their own feed. People say land is plentiful in Oregon, so we shouldn't have any problems if we don't rush."

"I agree," Pa says. "The newspapers say Oregon has lots of beautiful land, and rain for our crops. And we have a lot to get done before we leave, so we could use a few weeks to prepare!"

For the next few weeks, you camp outside town and prepare for your journey. You spend your days helping Pa ready the wagon, or with Ma going to shops to buy food, clothes, and camping supplies. Ma haggles over the prices of everything from matches to shoelaces.

"Whoa! Look at that!" Samuel says, pointing to a gigantic canvas sack of flour.

"It says it weighs a hundred pounds," Ma says. "That's heavier than you or Hannah!"

FLOUR

100 LBS

You're in Wyatt's General Store. The friendly storekeeper piles all your goods in a corner.

"We'll need bacon," Ma says. Your eyes open wide as the storekeeper weighs a fifty-pound slab of fatty bacon. You've never seen one so enormous.

"Won't it spoil?" you ask.

"Nope," the shopkeeper says. "I pack it with bran, which keeps the fat from melting. It'll stay fresh for months."

You point to a brown patty. "What's that?"

"Those are compressed vegetables," the shopkeeper says proudly. He explains that the vegetables are thinly sliced, then squeezed until all the liquid comes out. "This makes a dried vegetable cake. When you're ready to eat it, you just break off a piece and add water."

Samuel wrinkles his nose. "Yuck!" You all laugh, but you can't help but agree with him.

You stare at the huge pile of flour, coffee, bacon, sugar, salt, and beans. Ma says you need to take *two hundred* pounds of food per person on the Trail. But you wonder how boring it will be to eat the same few things every day.

Before you know it, it's time to set off on the journey. The ten-foot-long wagon is almost fully loaded now. Besides the food, it's full of spare parts, like extra wheels and a wagon cover. There's a water barrel, too, and some farming tools, cooking pans, tin dishes, and cups. The matches are stored in a watertight bottle. You also have a tent, and layers of woolen clothes and blankets to keep everyone warm and dry. Almost every inch of space in the wagon is used.

"Tomorrow's the big day," Pa says, "and it looks like we still have $42 left to spend on supplies." You started out with $1,000 Pa saved up from working long hours over the past year.

"What else should we get with the extra money?" you ask.

"More food," says Ma. "We don't want to run out."

"More spare parts for the wagon," says Pa, at the same moment. "In case something breaks while we're on the road."

They look at each other.

"How about some of those compressed vegetables?" Ma says. "We could use the vitamins. Or some cornmeal to make our meals more interesting, or molasses for cooking sweeter desserts."

"We could use an extra wheel and axle for the wagon," Pa responds. "And you can never have enough spare bolts."

What should you buy with the extra money?

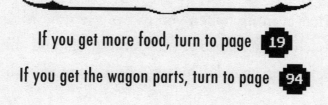

If you get more food, turn to page **19**

If you get the wagon parts, turn to page **94**

You decide to tell the captain of the wagon train what you saw. The next day, as you hike along, you ask to talk to him.

"Of course," he says in a friendly tone. As you speak, he listens carefully, taking you seriously.

"Thank you for telling me," he says. All day you see him talk to other people. You guess he's asking if they have seen or heard anything, too.

That evening, when you camp, the wagon captain approaches the man. He says something, and the man's face turns red. They end up yelling at each other.

It makes you nervous to watch, and you're shocked by how angry they are. *What have I started?*

That night, while you're in your tent, you hear loud voices right outside.

"How dare your little brat accuse me of stealing!" the man bellows furiously.

"Hold on now," Pa says. "Let's not get too excited."

"Yes, please," Ma says. "We don't want any trouble. We were just being extra careful."

"Well, I suggest you be careful somewhere else," the man says in a threatening tone. "This wagon train isn't for you. I was checking the bolts on everyone's wagon wheels, making sure the wheels are safe."

You've been kicked out of the train because of your suspicion and mistrust. There's safety in

numbers out here on the prairie, but now your family is left alone to fend for yourselves.

Pa looks at you with a sad expression as the rest of the wagon train pulls away. It's a long way to Oregon.

☞ **THE END**

You turn as quickly as you can and start to run.

"Get back to camp!" you shout to Hannah and Samuel, who scurry away.

As you start to follow, you see something small moving in your path. It's a bear cub! You pause, uncertain of where to turn.

Just then, you feel a terrible pain through your leg, and you fall to the ground. The grizzly has caught up to you and slashed you with her claws!

"OW!" you scream. You scramble to your feet and grab a big branch. You swing it at the bear, then run in the opposite direction as fast as you can.

Your leg is throbbing, but you keep moving. Luckily, the bear has reached her cub, and she ignores you now.

Once you're certain you aren't being chased, you stop.

Panting and wheezing, you look down at your leg. You can't see much in the dark, but your clothes are torn, warm, and wet. You must be bleeding.

You limp back into camp, and someone yells when they see you. Ma and Pa come running over.

"Did . . . Hannah . . . and . . . Samuel?" you pant.

"Yes, they are okay," Ma says. "Oh, no! Your leg!"

"And Archie?" you ask.

"Archie is fine," Pa says. "What happened?"

"Bear," you say.

Everyone gasps. The bear attacked! You tell them what happened.

"Bears usually leave people alone," Caleb says. "She must have been protecting her cub."

Pa takes a closer look at the wound. Ma cringes and looks away. The cuts are deep, and you can almost see your leg bone in one place.

"Let's clean this and wrap it up," Pa says.

As Pa pours alcohol over the wound, you faint from the stinging. When you wake up, your wound is wrapped in a clean cloth, but it feels like it's burning. The pain is almost intolerable.

For the next few days, you ride in a sling hung between two oxen. The pain doesn't get better, and the wound doesn't heal. Instead, it swells, oozes, and turns black and purple.

Your wagon train doesn't have any doctors. But everyone who sees your leg thinks the infection is bad.

"I think we have to amputate," you overhear Caleb say to Ma.

"No!" Ma gasps. "I won't let my child lose a leg."

"But look at the leg. He may die if we don't cut it off." Caleb is whispering but you can still hear him.

"But we can't perform surgery here, out on the Trail without a doctor," Ma says. "It's filthy!"

You feel faint and everything seems to be spinning. When you come to, Pa is looking at you.

"Your leg is in bad shape," he says as he fights tears. "I think we should ask the vet to help us operate now, before the infection spreads, but Ma thinks we should try something else."

"What else is there?" you ask, trying to be brave.

"She thinks we can go to the Otoe people, and ask for traditional medicine. But we don't know if it will work. If the infection spreads, you could lose more than a leg."

You pause.

Do you agree with Ma or Pa?

If you agree to surgery, turn to page **109**

If you go to a Otoe healer, turn to page **138**

I *should suck out the venom, if I can,* you decide. You're dizzy and your heart is racing, so it takes you a minute to pull out your pocketknife. You make a little X-shaped cut over the bite, but your vision is blurry so you have to concentrate. You don't know which hurts worse, cutting your skin or the bite itself. You quickly put your mouth over the cut, and suck as hard as you can. Then you spit out whatever is in your mouth, but it just looks and tastes like blood.

Your arm is throbbing from the pain. You race back to camp, yelling, "I've been bitten by a snake!"

Ma's face turns white and she rushes over to you. Blood is dripping down your arm.

"Show me the bite," she says. "Why is there so much blood?"

"I tried to suck out the venom," you say, as you start to feel dizzy.

Ma cleans the wound and then wraps it with a cloth. But what you both don't know is you have made the problem worse. When you tried to suck out the venom, you raised your arm above your heart, which helped spread the venom through your body. Running to get back to camp was a bad idea, too.

You start to feel chills, and soon you have a fever. Then comes nausea, and your vision blurs. Finally, you have trouble breathing. You lie down, trying to focus on your mother's face.

Your eyes are closing and you can't stay awake. You have glimpses of Ma slapping your face to keep you awake. Finally, you can't fight anymore. It's all over.

☞ **THE END**

You tie a thick rope to the back of your wagon. If people pull on it from behind, it will slow the wagon as it goes down the hill. Pa checks the rope, making sure it's tight.

Then he says, "Let's lower her down!"

"Can I help?" you ask Pa.

"Okay," Pa says, smiling. "But hold on in the back where it's safe."

It feels like a giant game of tug-of-war. Pa and two other strong men hold the rope tightly. And then you grab the end.

"On a count of three," Pa says.

You tense your muscles. When Pa shouts "THREE," you pull back with all your strength as Pa releases the brake on the wagon wheels. A sudden force yanks you forward, and makes you lose your footing on the sandy hill. The rope burns your hands so badly, you let go and fall to the ground.

Then one of the men loses his grip, and releases the rope. Pa and the last man pull with all their might. But the wagon starts to drag them down the hill. Faster and faster it rolls, until finally they have to let go, too. The wagon continues to speed down the hill until . . . *CRASH!*

It lands in a wrecked heap.

You rush down the hill. The wagon has broken into pieces, and two of the wheels have fallen off. Supplies lie all over, and a big flour sack has torn apart. White powder covers everything.

"Our wagon!" Pa cries.

Feeling anxious and scared, you look at all your family's possessions lying in piles on the ground. Your heart sinks. But then you can't help but notice your surroundings. Ash Hollow is breathtaking, vibrant, and bright green. A flowing spring is circled by tall cedar trees, and there are flowers and fruit bushes everywhere. It's so peaceful that suddenly even your crashed wagon looks a little better.

Maybe it wouldn't be such a bad thing to be stuck in this beautiful spot for a while, you think.

Ma, Hannah, and Samuel are staring around Ash Hollow in amazement. You can tell they feel the same way as you. But Pa is too upset to notice anything but the wagon.

Do you quietly help him fix up the wagon, so you can get back on the Trail? Or do you try to convince him that you should stay where you are for a while?

If you work to fix the wagon, turn to page **87**

If you convince Pa to stay, turn to page **43**

I don't feel well, Ma," you say.

Ma looks at you with concern and puts a hand on your forehead.

"You're burning up," she says. "Go lie down."

As you drift back to sleep, you see Ma and Pa talking with Caleb outside your tent. Caleb looks at you, and then gently nods his head.

When you wake up, you throw up over and over again. You don't stop until, finally, nothing is left to come out.

"Ughhh." You moan and roll over.

Pa brings you some murky water to drink. *Bleh!* It's salty and bitter, and it makes you gag again. But Pa stands sternly over you until you drink it all. Then you fall back asleep. He wakes you after a few hours and gives you more of the nasty water.

When you wake up again, you're still sweating, but not as much as before.

"Do you feel better?" Hannah asks, peeking into the tent.

"Yeah, a little," you say, weakly. Ma comes in,

smiling with relief. She says your fever has broken. Pa brings you a cup of soup flavored with buffalo bones that has potatoes in it. It tastes really good, and you're able to keep it inside you.

The next morning you hit the Trail again. You're still too weak to walk, so you ride in the wagon. The sway of the oxen rocks you to sleep, but every now and again, you go over a big bump that jolts you awake. *Ouch!*

After a few days, you finally arrive at a military outpost called Fort Kearny. It's pretty basic, but it's a good place to rest after the last three weeks. There are dozens of wagons parked around the buildings, and you see lots of soldiers.

At the fort, you visit a doctor, who confirms you have dysentery.

"It was wise to rest and drink lots of liquids," he says. "Many people on the Trail don't survive dysentery, because if they can't keep anything down, they get dehydrated. We suspect it comes from unclean food and water."

By the next day, you feel a lot better. You walk over to Eliza's tent with Samuel and Hannah.

"I've been waiting for you," Eliza says with a grin.

"I want to show you something." She leads you and the other kids around the side of the main building. There are a bunch of chickens running around. Eliza crouches down and cups something in her hands. *Cheep!* Resting in her palms is the tiniest, fuzziest chick you've ever seen.

"It's so cute!" Hannah coos, stroking the chick.

Just then, a soldier with a stubbly beard walks up. He smiles and asks where your wagon captain is. You notice he is filthy and smells bad, and you step back. But you introduce him to Caleb.

After supper that night, you hear a lot of arguing around the campfire.

"What's going on?" you whisper to Joseph. He shrugs and shakes his head.

Later, Caleb explains to Ma and Pa that the soldier is working as a guide. He wants to lead your wagon train to Oregon. He says he knows a special path that can get you there a month early. But to do so, he's asking for a lot of money as payment.

"I don't think it's wise to stray off the Oregon Trail," Caleb says, shaking his head. "But a month is really tempting. Some families are planning to leave our wagon train, to follow the guide. It's up to you to stick with us or go with them."

You look at Pa nervously. You don't want to leave Joseph and Eliza. But it would be great to get to Oregon sooner. You see Ma's forehead wrinkle. She is thinking hard, too.

What does your family decide to do?

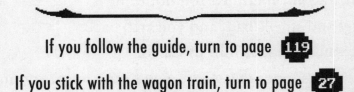

If you follow the guide, turn to page **119**

If you stick with the wagon train, turn to page **27**

I think we can get rid of some things," you say quickly. You look down, not wanting to see if you've disappointed Pa.

"It's okay. We overpacked," Pa says. "Let's see what we don't need."

You feel a flood of relief that Pa isn't upset with you for wanting to rest.

"Let's start with the heaviest things we can think of," Ma says. "I can do without this extra cast-iron skillet. I don't need two."

"I don't need all of these farming tools," Pa adds.

"We can throw away my doll," Hannah offers. She grips the raggedy cloth doll tightly.

"You keep that, Hannah," Ma says kindly. "It doesn't weigh much." Everyone had been allowed one toy or special thing from home, and Ma insists you keep those. But you do find plenty of other things you agree you can live without.

You start throwing some extra things off the side of the wagon. Other families in your wagon train do the same. Soon the Trail is littered with objects.

"Maybe someone will come by and find these things useful," Pa says, shaking his head at all the discarded items.

When you're finished, the wagon is lighter. The oxen seem happier, too. Caleb sends someone ahead to scout for a nice spot to camp. Everyone parks their wagons in a circle, called a "corral." He says it will keep the animals safe and prevent a stampede.

You think the oxen look too tired to stampede anyway. It's your turn to give them feed while everyone else sets up camp. You pet an ox, and he looks at you with big, brown eyes.

"Every time you have dinner, you'll have less feed to carry," you tell him.

At night, when you're sound asleep in your tent, you hear a loud noise. It's the guard Caleb assigned to watch over the camp! He yells and sounds the alarm. Pa scrambles to get out of the tent.

Bandits!

A group of rough-looking men has ridden into the corral. Your heart pounds as they tie up all the grown-ups. And then they rob you. It looks like the

trail of stuff you left led them right to you! Luckily, no one gets hurt. But now you're left with nothing.

No one has any supplies, and there is no sign of water or food in sight. Things are looking pretty bleak. It's every wagon for itself as you go your separate ways and abandon the Trail.

☞ **THE END**

You help Pa empty the supplies out of the wagon. Then he surveys the damage.

"We'll need to replace all these broken boards," he says, sounding glum. "And fix the wheels."

Luckily, you brought extra wagon parts with you when you left Independence, which come in handy now. And Pa is a skilled carpenter. He cuts down several of the cedar trees that fill Ash Hollow. Then he is able to make smooth planks out of them to fix the wagon.

Finally, after three days of working around the clock, your wagon is back in order, and looks almost as good as new. Pa watches proudly as you all admire it. You load your stuff back on the wagon, and you're ready to hit the Trail again.

You're sad to leave Ash Hollow, but you're looking forward to seeing Courthouse Rock and Jail Rock. Ma has told you all about the incredible rock formations. She's heard they are hundreds of feet tall!

But after a week of travel, you start to get the

feeling something is wrong. You're sure you've seen this part of the Trail already.

"Pa, I think we have already been through here," you say.

"No, it's all starting to look the same to you," Pa laughs. "We've been on this Trail a long time!"

You stay quiet, but start to pay closer attention. You're certain that tree with the giant branch on the ground was there yesterday. Caleb has led you in a giant circle!

"Caleb?" you ask him.

"Yes," he says.

"Um . . . I think we've been going in a circle for the past two days."

"What? How?"

"I'm seeing the same landmarks," you explain.

"Listen," Caleb says, patting you on the shoulder. "I've got my compass and it's never failed me. It's impossible that it's wrong. We're fine."

You try to tell yourself that Caleb's the one who knows best. But then, you see wagon ruts that are

leading in a different direction. You're pretty sure they are from a wagon train that was going the *right* way!

Do you try again to convince Caleb that he's lost? Or do you tell the others and show them the ruts?

If you try to convince Caleb, turn to page **53**

If you tell the others, turn to page **59**

You decide to continue on the Trail after two brief days of rest. No one wants the wagon train to leave without you, but you worry about your oxen. Healthy livestock mean the difference between success and failure on the Oregon Trail. You just hope you'll find green grass soon.

"Now that the wagon is lighter, it'll be easier for the oxen to pull," Pa says.

But neither the lighter load nor the rest seems to help. Once you're back on the Trail, everyone is grumpy and Pa's optimism fades. Hannah and Samuel complain constantly about how tired they are. They take turns sitting on the bumpy wagon, but that doesn't help much.

The team of oxen grows weaker. Frustrated, Pa even tries driving them with a whip, which he hates doing. But the animals just get more exhausted and move even slower. The wagon train has to take lots of breaks so the animals can rest. And Pa gives your team so much extra feed, you're starting to run out.

After a couple days, the oxen refuse to move at all. Pa pushes and tugs them. He pets them and talks to them. He promises them green grass if they'll just keep going. But they won't budge.

You've never seen Pa so worried.

The oxen eventually die. They're so thin they're not even useful as food. Now your wagon train is stranded on the prairie. Ma and Pa decide that going on isn't possible. Your best bet is to start walking back to Independence to set up a new life there. At least you tried.

☞ **THE END**

You decide to wait for the rain to stop. Your family huddles under the wagon cover, with Archie curled in a ball at your feet. The rain continues to relentlessly pelt the top of your wagon.

By the time night falls, it's too muddy to camp. You all squeeze into the wagon, but it's hard to fall asleep with Samuel's elbow stuck in your back, and with tin cups clanging every time you move.

"Hannah! Move your feet!" Her toes are pressed into your forehead. *Yuck!*

You climb out of the wagon. Getting wet is better than being cramped any longer or sleeping, you decide. You shiver all night.

Finally, the clouds break the next day. You take a nap, then help Ma spread out wet clothes to dry.

Pa finds the least muddy spot to set up camp. He

manages to start a fire with dried buffalo poop, called "buffalo chips," and you enjoy a hot meal for the first time in a while.

Over the next few days, the ground slowly dries up. The following morning, Caleb says it's time to head out again.

Pa touches the oxen gently with his whip. They start to pull, and suddenly you hear a terrible grinding sound. *POP!* The back of the wagon drops. You know what's happened before anyone says anything. The mud around the wheels dried, trapping the wagon in place. The rear axle bent. And the wheels snapped off.

Three other wagons break apart, too. That's way too much to fix on the prairie. So you load as much as you can onto the remaining three wagons. This gets you to the next trading post, but you won't get to Oregon without a wagon of your own.

☞ **THE END**

All stocked up with the extra wagon parts, you begin your trip. Your wagon train has eleven wagons, and the captain is a man named Caleb. He's really nice, so you've all voted for him to be in charge. He decides when the wagons start and stop each day, where to camp, and what order the wagons travel in. He also assigns the guards each night.

The only problem with Caleb is that his oldest son, Joseph, acts like he knows everything. He brags all the time, so you avoid him as much as you can. Caleb's daughter, Eliza, is close to your age and easier to be around.

As your wagon train rolls out of town, you can't believe you're really on the Oregon Trail! That feeling of excitement carries you through the first day of walking. But over the miles, your feet and legs start to ache. The thrill of walking fifteen miles a day fades quickly.

By the end of the first week, you are wishing for your house back in Kentucky. Sleeping in the tent is uncomfortable, not like your bed back home. But no one else complains, so you stay quiet. At least your

family has a tent. Some families sleep outside under the stars.

The next couple of weeks are filled with long days. Most of the time, you walk beside the wagon. Six strong oxen are pulling the load, but it's heavy even for them. Riding in the wagon is bumpy and there's hardly any room. But sometimes, when you feel like you can't take another step, you jump aboard for a break and dangle your tired feet off the edge.

"My stomach aches," says Samuel, as he trudges along beside you. Your little brother hasn't been eating much the past few days, and looks like he's lost weight. Every day it's the same kind of food. Breakfast is johnnycakes or cornmeal mush and bacon. Supper is trail beans, more bacon, and soda biscuits. Samuel says the biscuits are too heavy, not like the fluffy ones Ma made back home when you had lots of milk and eggs.

You wonder what Ma might have bought if you and Pa hadn't wanted to bring wagon parts instead. Some molasses pudding would really hit the spot.

You've seen Archie, your dog, chasing a few jackrabbits along the Trail. Maybe what Samuel needs is a nice, hot rabbit stew for supper. You could try to catch a rabbit with his slingshot.

Joseph has already caught rabbits for his family. You've seen him walk by carrying the rabbits, and looking pleased with himself. But you don't want to ask him for help. He might act like even more of a show-off than he is already.

You look at your wagon. You'd probably get a good view, and a better shot at the rabbits, if you stood up on its side. But with all the bumping, it's hard to stay balanced.

Do you swallow your pride and ask Joseph to help you catch a rabbit? Or do you try to catch your own rabbit?

**If you ask Joseph to help you catch a rabbit,
turn to page 103**

**If you try to catch a rabbit on your own,
turn to page 23**

A guide sounds like the right choice. He knows
the Trail better than any of you, and he can help to
catch food and keep you safe. The Osage man's name
is Black Bear. He hands the molasses and syrup to a
small boy. Pa has also given Black Bear some bacon
and a quilt Ma sewed.

You head back on the Trail and walk with Black
Bear. He knows a lot about nature, and shows you
different birds and plants along the way.

"This one is good to eat," he says, breaking off a
leaf and chewing it. "But don't touch that one." He
points to a plant with red berries. "It's bad for you."

Then, suddenly, your wagon goes over a big
bump. You hear a grinding *CRUNCH*.

"Halt!" Pa yells to the oxen. He runs to the back
of the wagon, and bends down to look under it.

"It's one of the axles," he says. His face grows
pale. "This is terrible! We didn't get extra ones."

You and Ma exchange a glance. Pa was right
about spare parts. An axle has snapped and can't
be fixed.

Black Bear helps you empty out your wagon. Luckily, Pa is a carpenter and is able to turn the wagon into a two-wheeled cart. It won't get you to the end of the Trail. But you can take just what you need to get back to Independence. Black Bear agrees to lead you there in exchange for an ox.

Pa walks like a man who has been broken, and it makes your heart ache to look at him. You hope your family can figure out a way to get to Oregon later.

☞ THE END

You decide to wait before you say anything to the captain of your new wagon train. Maybe if you keep an eye on him, you'll get a better idea of what the mysterious man is up to. The experience with the soldier stealing money is making you more nervous than usual. You don't know who to trust anymore.

You keep an eye on the man all day. Whenever he looks at you, you look away and pretend to be doing something else. You notice he usually carries a box.

What could the box be for?

Then, you spot him creeping up to yet another wagon. You quietly move closer, to watch him crouch down by a wagon wheel. He slowly opens up his box.

Aha! you think. *I'm going to catch him stealing!*

Then suddenly, he turns around and notices you.

"Hey there!" the man says. "Could you possibly give me a hand?"

You see that he is holding a tool, and it looks like he is trying to tighten a bolt on the wagon wheel.

Embarrassed, you realize he isn't stealing anything after all. He's just trying to keep everyone safe.

"I . . . uh . . . need to get some firewood," you say, not wanting to admit you were suspicious of him. You head over to the forest, and reach for a pile of branches. You realize you were too quick to suspect him, but you don't have much time to feel bad about it before . . .

YOW! You feel a sudden, intense pain on your forearm. Then something long slithers away, its tail and rattle disappearing under a branch.

You've been bitten by a snake!

You feel faint and numb. Rattlesnakes are

common in these parts, and they are poisonous and deadly. You need to think fast, but you feel weak, and your eyes feel heavy. Do you try to suck out the venom and spit it out? Or do you keep your arm very still, and walk slowly back to camp?

If you suck out the venom, turn to page **73**

If you keep your arm still, turn to page **134**

Hey, Joseph. Could you use Samuel's slingshot to help me catch a rabbit?" You speak quickly, keeping your eyes on the ground.

"Nope," Joseph says. You feel hot inside and wish you'd never said anything to him.

Then he adds, "That's because I don't use a slingshot to catch rabbits."

You look up.

"Then how do you do it?" you ask.

"I use traps," he says. "Let me show you."

Surprised, you agree.

That evening, while the others make camp, Joseph shows you how to bait his traps. A few hours later, you catch a big jackrabbit. Pa skins it, and soon it is simmering in a pot.

Your family invites Joseph's over for rabbit stew at suppertime. Eliza adds some herbs she found to the pot, and they make the stew extra delicious. Samuel happily eats two helpings. He grins as he uses soda biscuits to mop up the last bits off his tin plate. He likes soda biscuits now that he's used to them.

"We make a good team," Joseph tells you later, around the campfire. He pulls some honey candy from his pocket and breaks you off a piece. You savor the sweetness. You're glad to have a new friend.

A few days later, your wagon train stops to camp by the Kansas River. You'll have to cross the rushing river to keep going. That will be tough, but for now, camping on the river is a nice break.

"Time to work, kids," says Ma. "Let's wash those filthy clothes."

You've been wearing the same clothes for almost a week, and the wagon train kicks up lots of dust. Whenever it's your turn to travel last, you always get covered in dirt.

You help fill your family's biggest pot with water from the river. Ma lights a fire and boils the water. Then she adds lye soap and the first set of clothes. You feel the heat as you help her stir the pot.

When the clothes are clean, Ma rinses them in a washtub of cold water. Samuel and Hannah take turns wringing them out. Then you all spread the clothes out on large rocks to dry.

Meanwhile, Pa and Caleb catch fish for supper, which Ma batters with cornmeal. As you enjoy the flaky fried fish, Caleb makes an announcement.

"We have two choices for crossing the river," he says. "We can ford it or we can use Papan's Ferry."

In order to ford the river, the wagons will have to be made as waterproof as possible. Then the men will drive the oxen across. And you'll have to wade or swim, depending on how deep the water gets.

"What if our stuff gets ruined?" you ask.

"That's a risk," Caleb admits. "We'll cross where the water is shallow, and seal up the wagons as best we can using tar and candle wax."

"Fording a river can be dangerous," he continues. "We'll be careful, and our best swimmers will go first to make sure it's safe. But the animals could get scared, and we might get cold. And some of the supplies could get wet or lost."

Then Caleb explains the safer way across the river: Papan's Ferry. The ferry is a log-platform boat that carries one wagon at a time. A ferryman moves the boat with a long pole, pushing the pole along the bottom of the river. A rope stretches across the river to help guide the ferry.

The Papan brothers charge $1 per wagon for the ferry trip across the river. That's a lot of money you could use at trading posts instead. Plus, you'll have to wait a few days to cross. There's a long line of other wagons ahead of you. That would delay you getting to Chimney Rock.

Five of the families in your wagon train vote to ford the river. The other five argue for Papan's Ferry. They point out that it is safer, and waiting will give the oxen time to rest and graze. Healthy livestock are important for success on the Trail. Plus, you would all get to rest, too!

Caleb turns to your family. "Well, it looks like your wagon is the tiebreaker," he says. "What do you all want to do?"

How do you vote?

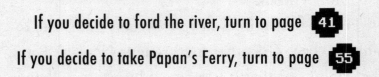

If you decide to ford the river, turn to page **41**

If you decide to take Papan's Ferry, turn to page **55**

Your voice quivers as you say, "Surgery, I guess." You glance at your diseased leg, then look away quickly. You want to be brave, and if you have to choose between life with one leg or dying here on the Trail, you'll take living.

A man from your wagon train will do the operation. He's a veterinarian, the closest thing you have to a doctor. He tries to keep you calm, and talks constantly as he gets ready. You don't hear anything he is saying. The man gives you some medicine that

makes you sleepy. The cling and clang of metal fills the air as the vet assembles his tools. You look around for Ma, and reach for her hand.

"I'm scared," you whisper. Pa walks over and grabs your other hand.

"I love you. You're going to be okay," Ma says, kissing your forehead.

You close your eyes. You bite down on a leather belt and wait for the pain. You feel like someone's ripping off your leg, and the agony is so bad that you pass out.

When you wake up, it's the next day. You're still dazed. You want to look down at your leg, but the thought is too scary. Pa gives you more medicine. Ma looks at you with tears in her eyes, but tries to be comforting. When you finally look down at your leg, you see bloody bandages on a stump.

The wagon train is forced to leave your family behind. Pa makes you some crutches, but even after weeks of rest, you can't move very fast with them. The pain still comes and goes. You have to stop often.

Your family travels alone back to the last trading post. From there, you'll slowly try to get back to Kentucky. Your journey on the Oregon Trail is over, but at least you survived.

 **THE END**

I think we can make it to the trading post, Pa,"
you say. Your heart sinks at the idea of more walking.
But you have months of long hiking days ahead. You
might as well get used to it.

"Good," Pa says, looking proud of you.

Samuel and Hannah look disappointed, but they
don't argue.

"I'll get you kids a treat when we arrive," Ma
promises you all.

Hannah perks up. "Can we get some honey
candy, please?"

"And some ice cream!" Samuel says.

A few days later, you arrive at the trading post.
Pa decides the family can spare some wagon parts,
tools, and half a sack of flour. In exchange, he gets
extra feed for the oxen to eat. The animals have been
getting thinner without grass to graze. Poor things!
You feed your favorite ox some grain from your hand.

Hannah and Samuel suck happily on their honey
candies. They make friends with some kids from
other wagons. An older boy organizes a game where

everyone kicks buffalo chips. Whoever makes these buffalo-poop patties go farthest is the winner.

You want to play, too, but you have to help Ma and Pa rearrange the wagon. Now that it is less full, you'll be able to take turns resting inside it when you're back on the Trail.

"I wonder if we should camp here for a few weeks," Pa says. "That way we can wait for the grass to grow a bit. We'd have to join another wagon train later, though."

"But there isn't much grass here for grazing in the meantime," Ma says. "What will the animals do while we wait?"

"The oxen will have to feed on the grain we have," Pa says.

"Would it be better to keep on going?" Ma asks.

"We can push on now," Pa says. "There might be greener pastures ahead."

You like the idea of resting for a while. Your legs are tired. But staying at the trading post means you'll lose time getting out West. And your wagon train will leave without you.

What does your family do?

**If you stay at the trading post for a few weeks,
turn to page 129**

**If you continue on the Trail now,
turn to page 90**

I think it's too late to climb higher," you say.

"I agree," says Eliza. "Let's head back down while it's still light out."

The three of you stop where you are to carve your names into the rock. You're glad you did, because by the time you climb down and get back to camp, the sun is setting. Ma looks relieved to see you.

"I was starting to get worried!" she says.

"The next landmark we'll see is Chimney Rock," says Pa. "It's supposed to be even more impressive."

Chimney Rock is the milepost you've been hurrying toward for weeks, and where the journey gets tougher. You decide to carve your name there, too. Maybe one day, when you're grown up, you'll come back to look for your carvings.

"We spotted a broken wagon while you were climbing," Samuel tells you as you sit next to him for a supper of beans and bacon. "It's nearby."

You look over at Pa. Maybe there's something useful in the deserted wagon.

"It's late, but can we go explore?" you ask.

"Yes, but don't go far," Pa says. "If you take too long, you'll be wandering around in the dark."

After supper, you head over to the deserted wagon with Samuel and Hannah. Archie happily runs after you. The broken wagon is almost completely empty, but you find a pail and some crates, and you start to look through them.

Just then, Archie sees a squirrel scampering by. He barks with excitement and dashes after it.

"Come back, boy!" you call after him. You chase him, calling his name.

A few moments later, you hear a muffled sound behind you.

"Archie," you say, turning around to scold him for running away. But it isn't Archie at all. You feel a scream rising in your throat.

You are face-to-face with a big grizzly bear!

You tremble, frozen in place. You hope Samuel and Hannah are far away.

You try to remember what Pa taught you about bears, as this one looks directly at you. *Are bears like*

dogs? you wonder. *If I run, will it chase me?* Or maybe you should just stand up straight and act unafraid. *If I do that, will it leave me alone?*

What do you do?

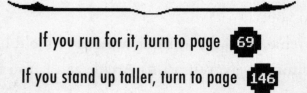

If you run for it, turn to page **69**

If you stand up taller, turn to page **146**

It will be nice to get to Oregon a month sooner," Ma says. "We could build our house while it's still warm out."

"Yes," Pa agrees. "And we'll save a lot of money, since we'll use fewer supplies along the way. We'll get better land, too!"

Your family and four others follow the soldier and his shortcut, leaving the rest of the wagon train. You're feeling pretty good about your decision now.

The soldier's name is Will, and he tells some great stories around the campfire. They're all about the Trail, and most of them end with him saving the day.

But on the third night of camp, Will says something strange to you right before bedtime.

"I never meant to do wrong by you people," he says, with a sad look. You don't know what that means or what to say, so you just nod and go to your tent, puzzled.

The next morning, you awaken to a lot of shouting outside.

"We've been swindled!" A man from another wagon yells.

"That crook!" says a woman, red in the face.

"What's going on?" you ask Ma.

"Will's gone," Ma says flatly. "He took our money and left us here."

"Are you sure?" You don't want to believe it. "Maybe he just went ahead to scout?"

"No. He left us," Pa says. "All his things are gone."

You remember what Will said to you last night. And then you know for sure he isn't coming back.

No one in the wagon train knows what direction to head in from here. And you are running out of drinking water. Will had promised you would reach a spring the next day.

"The water barrel is almost empty," Pa says. Your throat is already feeling dry.

"I saw a little pond," Hannah says, pointing back in the direction of yesterday's hike.

"Let's go check," Pa says to you.

You and Pa carry some empty barrels to the pond. The water is almost still and a little murky, and it smells a bit rotten. You see branches and leaves floating in it.

"It's okay. We'll clean it," Pa says. He stuffs some grass and moss into a barrel, then pours the pond water in after it.

"See how the grass traps the dirt?" he says. Next, he pours the water through a handkerchief to filter out even the smallest particles.

"There," Pa says, looking proud of himself. "Clean water." You're amazed at how clear the water looks now.

You take the barrels back to camp and show Ma. "Maybe we should boil it before drinking it," she says. But boiling it means building a fire first. And then you will have to wait for the water to cool. The water looks refreshing. And you are so thirsty.

If you drink some of the water before Ma boils it,
turn to page **30**

If you wait until Ma boils the water,
turn to page **38**

You race back toward camp as quickly as you can. When you get close to the circle of wagons, you see the man Caleb assigned as tonight's guard.

You're out of breath from running, but you still manage to sputter out a few words.

"Boy . . . taking . . . ox!"

"Thieves?" The guard looks at you with alarm.

While you try to catch your breath, the guard fires his rifle in the air, twice. That's the signal to tell everyone the camp is under attack!

"Wait a minute!" you protest. "I didn't say we are being attacked."

"Didn't you just say local people are stealing oxen?" the man asks you with a frown.

"Yes," you say. "But it was just a boy and only a single ox. Not really an attack."

But the guard doesn't want to hear what you just said. "It doesn't matter who it is or how many. If they're taking our animals, that's an attack!"

You follow the guard back to camp, where all

the men are getting ready for battle and preparing to march to the Lakota-Sioux settlement.

You run to your father. "What is it?" Pa asks. "What happened?"

You tell Pa about the boy leading the ox away.

"I thought he was stealing it," you say. "But maybe he didn't know it was ours."

Pa looks at you carefully.

"This is my fault, Pa," you say. "One ox isn't a reason to start a fight." You feel your heart pounding in your chest, and want to cry.

"Let's just go over there to talk to them," Pa says. "And get our ox back. You come with me."

You head over to the Native American settlement with Pa and the other men. Caleb and the guard lead the way. Something about the way everyone is talking loudly and waving their fists makes you feel scared. It looks to you like they want to start a fight, not talk about a missing ox.

When you get there, you see a large group of Lakota-Sioux people. They all gather together, and stare at you all charging in uninvited. They are looking at your group's rifles. Little kids run away and hide behind their mothers' legs.

A Lakota-Sioux man walks up with a serious look on his face. "Where's the ox?" the guard asks him. The two men stand chest-to-chest and stare at each other.

"Do you see the boy?" Pa whispers to you. You just shake your head, because you don't see him anywhere, and you don't see your ox, either. What if the boy doesn't even live here?

BANG! Someone fires a rifle, and then you hear another. You look helplessly at Pa.

"Run for cover!" he shouts.

You rush in the direction of the nearest tree to hide. But a full-blown battle has started. By the time it's over, you will lose half of the wagon train.

☞ **THE END**

You decide to play it safe and travel diagonally across the river, even though you'll have to be cold for longer. It's much easier to move along with the current instead of fighting it. Pa steers the animals with your help. The water comes up to your waist, and it sure is chilly! Ma watches from the wagon where she's riding with Samuel and Hannah.

You safely wade across the river, and no one in the wagon train loses any animals or wagons. But you and Pa are completely soaked and shivering, and your teeth won't stop chattering. Even sitting by the campfire wrapped in a blanket doesn't warm you up.

But the worst is yet to come. The next day, you

start to feel queasy. First you have stomach cramps, then you have diarrhea that seems like it will never stop. Next, you start throwing up over and over. You feel weak, you're incredibly thirsty, and your legs start to ache. Finally, you have a fever and can't keep your eyes open.

"I think that river was tougher than we wanted to think it was," Pa tells Ma. They both look concerned.

Then the same thing starts to happen to Samuel and Hannah.

Next, it's Ma's and Pa's turn.

You didn't get sick from the river. You have cholera, a contagious disease you get from unclean water or food. You've heard stories of entire families who were wiped out in a day or two on the Trail. You and your family are among the unlucky ones.

☞ THE END

Your family decides to make camp at the trading post for the next few weeks. You realize now it was a mistake to leave Independence so early. It would have been wiser to wait until May.

Other wagon trains arrive at the trading post every day. The travelers look as exhausted as you were when you got here. They bring extra goods to trade for feed for their oxen. Sometimes they just give away supplies because they don't want to carry the weight.

You, Samuel, and Hannah set up a lemonade stand for the other travelers, using cider vinegar in place of lemons. Ma sells quilts and washes clothes for a fee. Pa trades goods and hunts buffalo, which he

dries into jerky strips and sells. Archie runs free on the prairie and plays fetch with anyone willing. It's a good life, and as the weeks pass, you grow less and less interested in leaving.

"Someone wants to buy our oxen for twice what I paid for them," Pa says one day. "With the money we get, we can afford to build a log cabin."

Ma looks at you.

"What do you think?"

There's plenty of land, and a good life right here. You have more space than you had in Kentucky, and it's quieter than Independence. The blisters on your feet have healed nicely. And no one wants new ones. You all decide you don't need to go any farther on the Oregon Trail.

☞ **THE END**

I *don't want to disappoint Ma,* you think. You don't want to slow everyone down, either. So you decide to push on, even though you don't feel well.

Ma doesn't notice when you slip Archie your cornmeal hash and bacon. He happily gobbles it up and wags his tail. You're glad he enjoys it, even though you can't bring yourself to eat anything.

Everyone packs up camp and heads out just like every morning. You walk alongside the wagon as usual, but soon find yourself falling behind.

"Hurry up!" Samuel says, running back to you. "You're moving so slowly today."

"Are you feeling okay?" Hannah asks, peering into your face. "You look kind of pale."

"My stomach hurts a little," you admit, as you try to walk faster. Your head aches too.

Then suddenly, a major cramp hits you. You double over in pain.

Ma runs over to you. You urgently feel diarrhea coming on. And you get the runs, over and over.

Pa gives you some salty water to drink. But you can't keep it down, and you throw up. Every time you take a sip, you have to vomit again.

"I'm scared," you say weakly. "What's wrong with me?"

"You're going to be okay," Ma says. But you see her exchange worried looks with Pa. The entire wagon train stops to make camp,

even though it's only midday. Everyone comes by to check on you, including Caleb. And all of them have different opinions about how to treat you, based on information from the guidebook or remedies from people they've known.

You try to drink water again, but you can't sit up anymore. Your head feels so heavy that you lie down and pass out, falling into a deep sleep. The next day is a haze of people fussing, but you don't have enough energy to open your eyes. Everything hurts, and you just want the pain to stop. Then, finally, it does because . . . you die of dysentery.

 **THE END**

You pull a bandanna from your pocket, and tie it tightly around the bite, like it's a bandage. You hold your arm very still against your side, and slowly walk back to camp. Even though you want to run and scream, you stay calm. You don't want to spread the venom through your body. If you don't move much, maybe it won't get into your bloodstream.

When you get to camp, Pa sees you and rushes over.

"What happened?"

"I was bitten by a snake, Pa," you say. Tears start to stream down your face. You're really scared and in a lot of pain. "What is going to happen to me?"

"You'll be okay," Pa says, even though he doesn't sound very sure of it. He signals to Ma to come over.

Pa looks at your bite, which is red now, and your arm, which is swollen. He wraps your wound even tighter than you did, and sits you down carefully. You lean against a wagon wheel. Ma puts her arms around you to keep you warm as you shiver with chills. You sit there and try to stay awake, but the pain is making you drowsy.

When you wake up, your stomach hurts and you throw up. Your arm is numb, but you are alive. The poison hasn't spread.

You survived a snakebite from a poisonous snake! Some people might feel extra powerful and brave after that. But not you! You develop an intense fear of all critters on the Trail. Even the sight of a tiny spider makes you scream and jump. Everyone tries to be patient with you at first. They keep telling you things will be fine. And then at some point, they just start to find you annoying.

Ma and Pa argue about whether it's worth continuing on the Oregon Trail. Ma tells Pa his dream is not worth the risk of losing one of their children.

You beg your parents to take you back home to

Kentucky. You miss being in a house, where walls protect you from things that bite or sting.

"I just want to go home," you plead.

Finally, Ma and Pa agree with you. Your family is going home.

☞ THE END

I want to try the traditional medicine," you say. You don't know whether it will help or not, but you have to try something. You can't stand the idea of losing your leg or having the painful surgery. You just hope the medicine works.

Caleb sends a scout to the settlement of the Otoe-Missouria tribe. He comes back with two men, one young and one much older. The younger man speaks to you in English, not his native language, which is Chiwere.

"My name is Doré. This is Wahre'dua. He is a very good healer and he will fix your leg."

The healer Wahre'dua looks at your leg, then speaks rapidly to Doré. Next, he pulls some herbs from a leather pouch, and starts crushing and mixing them in a wooden bowl. Doré gathers more plants, which the healer pounds into a paste. He speaks to Doré in the Chiwere language, which you do not understand.

Finally, the healer spreads the paste gently all over your wound. It feels cool and soothing. You close your eyes and concentrate. *Anything to help it work,* you think.

Doré gives the rest of the paste to Ma. He tells her she needs to put it on your leg every day. Ma smiles at him gratefully, and as payment, she gives the healer a quilt that she's been working on for months.

You and Ma apply the paste for the next three days. By the third day, the redness and oozing of your wound is gone. The medicine is working!

Within a week, your leg is healing nicely, and it looks like it will be okay. Doré, Wahre'dua, and other Otoe people come back to check on you, and you happily show them how much better your leg looks. You'll probably have a huge scar for the rest of your life, but will gladly live with that in exchange for keeping your leg.

The wagon train gets ready to leave again. But Ma doesn't want to go with them.

"Look how amazing life is here," she says. "Let's ask to stay and find out more about these medicines."

Pa agrees. He wants to learn many things from the Otoe, too.

You ask to stay and live life with the Otoe people for a few weeks. They are wary. White emigrants have spread disease amongst other indigenous people. After careful consideration, the Otoe people welcome you to their land. You're going to take a break from the Oregon Trail and settle right here next to your new friends. Maybe you'll become a healer yourself one day.

☞ **THE END**

Hey!" you call out to the boy. He jumps a bit, startled.

"It's okay," you say, smiling and holding up your hands. "I think you have my ox."

The boy smiles back at you. He has dark eyes that sparkle and make him seem like he's about to laugh. He walks over to you and points to the ox, then he points at you.

You nod firmly.

"It's mine," you say, pointing to yourself.

The boy looks at the ox, then hands you the rope.

"Thank you," you say. The boy smiles again and runs off. You realize the ox must simply have strayed away

from camp, and you feel guilty for thinking the boy was a thief. You promise yourself to be less mistrustful out here on the Trail.

Two days later, it's finally your wagon's turn to ride Papan's Ferry. The breeze feels great against your face, but the ride is over quickly. On the far bank, you wait a few hours for the other ten wagons of your group to cross the river. And then, you all get back on the Trail again.

You start off, rested and refreshed. But after another week of constant walking, you become tired again. You're sick of the dust and the smell of sweaty oxen. The blisters on your feet are stinging, and your head aches a little, too.

"Push on a little farther," Caleb says to you, as if he is reading your mind. "I've read in my guidebook that we have a reward waiting, just ahead."

You smile weakly at Caleb's attempt to cheer you up, look down, and keep trudging along. Suddenly, you hear Ma gasp. Looking up, you see ahead a beautiful waterfall gushing down a cluster of rocks. You, Hannah, and Samuel race over to it, and sip water directly from the spring. The water is crystal clear and as cold as melted ice.

"This is Alcove Spring," Pa says with a smile. He washes his hands and face, and then he splashes water on you. You splash back, and you both laugh.

Alcove Spring is the prettiest place you have seen on the Trail so far. Lush green grasses and trees surround the waterfall. You overhear Eliza tell Joseph she wishes they could stay here forever.

You make camp by the waterfall, and the sound of the water lulls you to sleep. But when you wake up, you aren't refreshed. You have a bigger headache than you had yesterday, and you are sick to your stomach. It feels like you're going to throw up.

At breakfast, you don't feel like eating your cornmeal hash. And the scent of bacon makes you feel queasy.

"Can't we stay here for another day?" Hannah pleads, pointing to the waterfall. "I want to play in the water some more."

"Me, too," adds Samuel. "I'm so tired of walking. Can't we just stay here and farm?"

"I'm sorry," Ma says. "We have to keep moving

with the rest of the train if we want to make it to Chimney Rock on time." She looks at you. "Right?"

Ma looks tired, too, and you know she wants your help getting everyone moving. You want to tell her you don't feel well, but you also don't want her to think you are making excuses.

Do you tell her you don't feel well, or do you just push on?

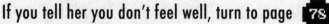

If you tell her you don't feel well, turn to page **78**

If you just push on, turn to page **131**

You force yourself to stand as straight and tall as you can in front of the bear. Your heart is pounding so hard the sound fills your ears. The bear is enormous, even on four legs, and her powerful body could easily crush you. One swipe from her paw could send you flying or worse. You get a glimpse of long curled claws that could tear through flesh.

The bear is staring straight at you, but you cast your eyes down instead of looking directly back. Your muscles tense and you fight the urge to run, backing up slowly and methodically.

"There, there, nice bear," you say softly. "I'm going to walk away now while you stay right there."

The bear doesn't move; she just watches you.

You keep inching backwards, facing her the whole time. Then suddenly, the bear stands up on two legs!

Your heart feels like it stops. *This is it,* you think as you close your eyes and wait.

But then, instead of attacking you, the bear drops back down to all fours again. She turns and ambles away into the forest, seemingly unconcerned with you.

Even so, you're still paralyzed with fear. Then you feel something brush you from behind. Startled, you jump. *"Ahh!"*

"It's just me," you hear Hannah whisper. "We were hiding in the bushes."

"That was so scary!" Samuel says from her side.

You can't speak. But you hold tightly to your sister's and brother's hands, and race back to camp.

Everyone is stunned by your story. They all talk about how brave you were. Ma holds you tight and covers you with kisses, while Pa congratulates you for thinking so clearly in a tense situation.

"That was close," Caleb says. "You were smart not

to try to fight the bear or run away. If you aren't a threat, most bears will leave you alone."

The next morning, when you set out on the Trail, the bear seems like a dream. You still can't believe you actually saw it.

"Pa told me we're not too far from Chimney Rock," Hannah says, walking next to you. She slides her hand into yours. You've been hearing about Chimney Rock since Missouri. The pioneers who have seen it say it's awe inspiring. The guidebook describes it as one of the wonders of the world.

"I see it!" Samuel shouts, pointing.

You catch a glimpse of the rock, still a day's hike away. Chimney Rock is a long, pointy rock that soars over three hundred feet high, like a giant pole sticking out of a haystack. The famous rock is more than just a landmark. It's the spot on the Oregon Trail where the prairie ends, and the rugged mountains begin. After this, your journey will get even harder.

Chimney Rock juts into the clear blue sky, so tall and skinny you don't understand how it doesn't fall

over! Everyone huddles together and stares at it. No one knows how it was formed.

"I've never seen anything like it," Pa says.

"It's even better than I'd imagined," Ma adds.

"We're so lucky to be here," Hannah says.

Everyone agrees. You *are* lucky to be here. You have been on an incredible journey and have had amazing adventures on the Trail. You've also made new friends, learned new skills, and have grown up a lot. Plus you've survived illness, and now you've even stood up to a bear!

You look at your family, so proud and determined. Pa looks back at you and smiles. His dream to own a farm is your dream now. And you're much closer to it than you were six weeks ago.

When you finally reach Chimney Rock, you and Pa carve your family's names into it. Now you've left one more mark along the Trail. As you look at your name etched in the stone, you wonder what other adventures lie ahead for you. Next your wagon train will trek through dangerous bluffs and famous forts, to a mysterious place called Devil's Gate. Your heart beats with excitement at the thought of the challenges still to come.

But I'm ready for them, you think with hard-earned confidence. *I'm a pioneer.*

 **THE END**

Chimney Rock

JUNE, 1850

GUIDE
to the Trail

LET'S EXPLORE!

You are about to embark on the journey of a lifetime, as one of the 400,000 adventurous and daring pioneers who trekked West between 1841 and 1870. You will be traveling 2,000 miles (3,200 kilometers) along the Oregon Trail with everything you need packed into a covered wagon. There will be adventures and dangers like you've never experienced before.

What do you have to look forward to when you get out West?

- A square mile of free land for your family to farm
- Plenty of rain for crops
- A chance to expand your nation to include ALL the land between the Atlantic and Pacific Oceans

Pack your wagon

Your ten-foot-long covered wagon will carry your supplies and the items you need for your new life in the Oregon Territory. There won't be room to ride in the wagon, so you'll walk alongside it. Choose carefully, and pack only what is most important. And don't overload your wagon!

You will need 200 pounds of food per person for the journey, mainly flour, bacon, sugar, cornmeal, fat, beans, rice, vinegar, baking soda, and citric acid. Don't forget essential building, farming, and wagon-repair tools. You should also take camping gear such as a tent, bedding, kitchen utensils, matches, and candles, as well as useful things such as rope, a pail, a rifle for hunting wild game, animal traps, and a first-aid kit.

Clothing should be woolen and shoes sturdy. Keep a bandanna in your pocket. Take buckskin for repairing shoes. Avoid the temptation to take luxury items, such as fancy foods, furniture, or nice clothes. Finally, it's important to buy a team of six healthy oxen to pull your wagon. They're slow animals, but they're reliable.

Join a
WAGON TRAIN

Pioneers will band together into wagon "trains," which are groups of wagons traveling together. Smaller groups are more manageable than large groups. The advantages of wagon trains include safety in numbers, helping each other with skills, and hunting together.

Wagon trains vote for a captain. His job is to decide when the wagons start in the morning, when they finish at night, and when to stop for lunch. He also assigns guards and decides what order the wagons travel in. No one wants to always travel at the end, breathing in the dust from the other wagons, so you will all take turns.

GO WEST

Choose the best time of the year to start your journey. If you start the Trail too early in the spring, there will not be enough grass for your oxen to graze. Leave too late and you risk reaching the mountains during the winter. Always move quickly, and try not to take shortcuts. Stick to the Trail!

Your days will start as early as four in the morning, with breakfast, chores, and loading your wagon. A bugle at seven means it's time to start the day's journey.

The wagon train will roll along until six p.m., except for an hour's lunch and rest time, called "nooning."

At the end of the day, you will unload your wagon, set up camp, take care of your livestock, and cook dinner. If you can't find firewood, you can burn buffalo-poop patties called "buffalo chips." Sometimes you sing or tell stories around the campfire. Everyone goes to sleep early, because it's hard work being a pioneer.

Challenges!

CROSSING RIVERS

You will have to cross rivers on the Oregon Trail. If they are shallow enough to ford, you can seal cracks in the wagons and drive your animal teams across. If the current is strong, it's best to cross diagonally.

ILLNESSES

Illnesses like cholera and dysentery are common on the Trail. No one understood germs in 1850, so one in ten travelers died. Try to keep your food and water clean, and if you get sick, rest and drink boiled liquids.

DESCENDING STEEP HILLS

When going down steep hills, lock the wheels of the wagon with ropes, chains, or built-in brakes. Then use your human strength or ropes to lower the wagon down the hill slowly. Be careful!

WEATHER

You will face extreme weather like rain, hail, snow, and heat during your trip. Besides staying safe, the next most important thing is keeping your wagon intact and your oxen healthy. Don't let the wagon wheels get stuck in mud.

ANIMALS

Keep your eyes open for wolves, black bears, prairie dogs, coyotes, and buffalo along the Trail. Some animals are shy, and you will seldom see them.

If you get bitten by a poisonous snake, stay still to prevent the venom from spreading. Trying to suck out the venom won't help. Grizzly bears are rare, but if you encounter one up close, don't run! Instead act unafraid and be non-threatening.

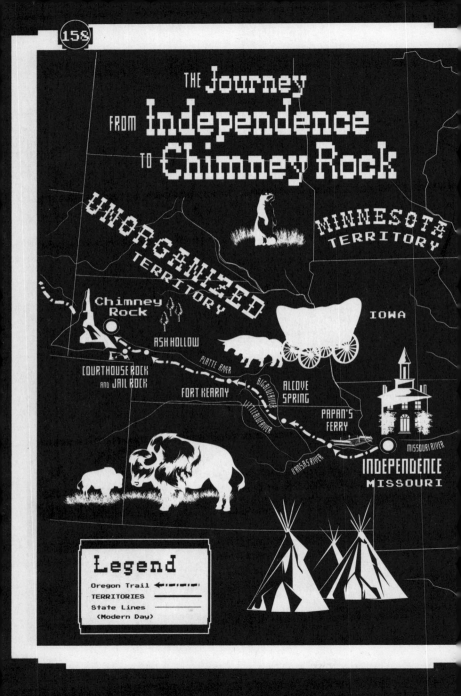

THE Journey FROM Independence TO Chimney Rock

UNORGANIZED TERRITORY

MINNESOTA TERRITORY

Chimney Rock

ASH HOLLOW

IOWA

PLATTE RIVER

COURTHOUSE ROCK AND JAIL ROCK

FORT KEARNY

BIG BLUE RIVER

ALCOVE SPRING

LITTLE BLUE RIVER

PAPAN'S FERRY

MISSOURI RIVER

KANSAS RIVER

INDEPENDENCE MISSOURI

Legend

Oregon Trail
TERRITORIES
State Lines
(Modern Day)

☞ FINDING YOUR WAY

In 1850, once you leave Missouri, there aren't roads or inns or restaurants or even states yet. The United States is made up of thirty states back East, but out West, you'll have to cross territories and Native American lands by using a compass, and by looking for famous landmarks.

The Trail itself is occasionally hard to see. Sometimes you can follow the tracks, called "ruts," left by other wagon trains. Other times those ruts might lead to abandoned forts or empty trading posts.

Look for these landmarks between Missouri and Chimney Rock

DISTANCE FROM INDEPENDENCE, MISSOURI:

PAPAN'S FERRY: 88 miles (142 km)

ALCOVE SPRING: 165 miles (266 km)

FORT KEARNY: 319 miles (513 km)

ASH HOLLOW: 505 miles (813 km)

COURTHOUSE ROCK & JAIL ROCK: 561 miles (903 km)

CHIMNEY ROCK: 575 miles (925 km)